D1314315

THE MESSAGE IN THE MIRROR

Written by: **Katrina Denise**   Illustrated by: **Fanny Liem**

The Message in the Mirror
Written by: Katrina Denise
Illustrated by: Fanny Liem

ISBN: 13: 978-0-692-84082-5

For Permission Request Contact:

Butterfly Speaks Publishing
Attn: Permission Request
Email: butterflyspeakspub@gmail.com

Dedication

This book is dedicated to my children who have
inspired me to write.
Mommy loves you, Jordan and Aria.

I also want to thank my parents, family, friends,
and former students who have encouraged me to
believe in myself,
and write stories about self-love and following your
dreams.

Your support has helped me to look in the mirror
and see a window of opportunity.

"No one loves me though I'm kind. I'll never be pretty or divine. Popular will I ever be, oh mirror, please tell me."

These were the words Aria said each day as she looked in the mirror, like the witch from her favorite story, Snow White. Aria would sit in front of the mirror wishing as the witch did, that she would be the prettiest and most liked girl.

Yet, each time she went to the mirror, the only images she could see along the sides were of others who teased her or who were more popular. There also was a hazy image in the center of the mirror that she couldn't quite make out. Aria always wondered who or what it might be.

One day while in the school lunchroom, Aria was tripped by Natalya, one of the prettiest and snobbiest girls in the school. Everyone laughed as Aria's food dripped on her clothes.

Natalya laughed as she said, "That girl is such a nerd."

"No," said Felicia, Natalya's best friend, "she's just plain old ugly. Look at her glasses, and old clothes."

The girls often taunted and teased Aria. Even though they got in trouble, it did little for Aria whose feelings had already been bruised.

That night when Aria got home, once again she stood in front of the mirror and said, "No one loves me though I'm kind. I'll never be pretty or divine. Popular will I ever be, oh mirror, please tell me."

Her hope was that the mirror would tell her that she was special or that she was pretty, but it didn't say or show anything except the faces of Natalya and Felicia and a fuzzy image in the middle.

The next day at school was no better than the previous day. Although Aria was a pleasant and friendly girl, there were a few classmates that she struggled to tolerate. Unfortunately, Albert, the class clown and prankster, was one of them. Aria usually tried to stay away from him.

Albert secretly had a crush on her, and the fact that she ignored him only made him mad. So to get back at her, he just made fun of her instead.

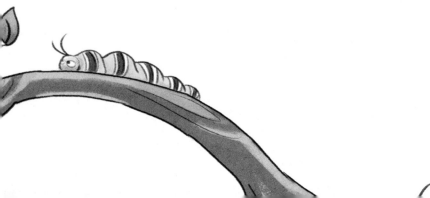

On this particular day, Albert not only threw paper at Aria, but he placed gum on her chair. Poor Aria walked around completely unaware of the gum stuck to her jeans. The other kids made fun of her behind her back, until finally, someone told her what happened.

Embarassed, she ran down the hall crying.

That afternoon Aria sat before the mirror once more and said, "No one loves me though I'm kind. I'll never be pretty or divine. Popular will I ever be, oh mirror, please tell me."

Aria soon went to sleep, wishing that she could simply escape it all.

The following week at school, Aria's teacher, Mrs. Coles passed out papers to the class, and announced that she received the highest score on a test. Aria thought to herself, "Now here's something else for everyone to tease me about."

" I don't like being smart," shouted Aria.

Mrs. Coles didn't understand and asked Aria to stay after class.

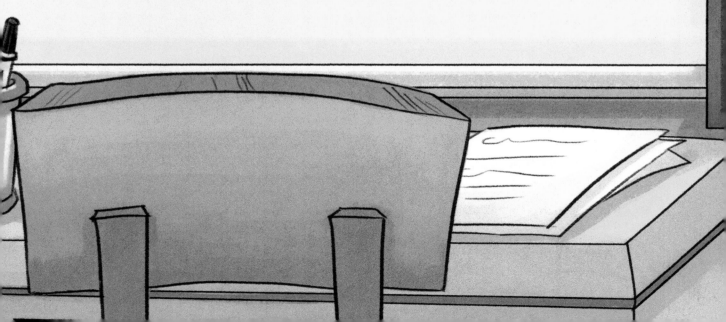

After class, Mrs. Coles asked Aria, "What seems to be the problem?"

Aria replied, "Nothing," in a solemn voice.

"There must be something wrong because you looked so upset even after hearing such great news," expressed Mrs. Coles.

Aria cried, "Everyone teases me for being smart and for the way that I look."

Her teacher said, "Aria, being smart makes you special, and it shows you have learned a lot. Ignore the comments of others and know that as long as you believe in yourself, you will always be beautiful and smart."

"Me, smart and beautiful?" Aria thought to herself, as if surprised to know that her teacher felt that way. In her mind, she wanted to be all of those things, yet somehow she doubted that could ever be true.

"Mrs. Coles, did you really mean what you said about me being beautiful and smart?" Aria asked cautiously.

"Why certainly," said Mrs. Coles. "You are also much cooler than those who tease you. It is never okay to put others down or tease them. Aria, your beauty shines even brighter, in the fact that you never treat others the same way they treat you."

As Aria walked home she smiled, as if she finally started to believe what her teacher said, that her beauty existed in many ways. Now she knew that being smart would allow her to be anything she wanted in life.

At home that evening, Aria went back to the mirror once again, hoping that it might say that she was pretty or popular. Again, she saw only the faces of those who teased her, Natayla, Felicia and Albert, and that fuzzy image in the middle, that she could not seem to figure out.

As she stared at the image, the mirror began to shake and the fuzzy picture became clear. Then the mirror finally answered and said, "Aria, you are both pretty and popular, and have been for some time. The problem was that you never believed it."

Aria listened attentively for she finally knew that the mirror was right.

"Aria," said the mirror, "True beauty comes from the inside and is about who you truly are. You are exactly what your teacher said, beautiful and smart."

When Aria went to bed that night her dreams were a little different. She didn't dream of being rescued, or trying to escape her problems.

She rested comfortably knowing that the message in the mirror was true. She was truly beautiful, and no one could ever change it.

Author's Note

Many children struggle with their self-esteem and self-worth. My hope is that young readers understand that each person is unique, and that there is enough room for each of us to shine.

Growing into the stars that we were born to be, requires a process or growth that is much like a butterfly. Throughout the book a caterpillar appears and eventually turns into a butterfly.

Talk with your child about this book, and see if he/she can identify the moment that Aria transforms and starts to truly shine.

You can also use this book to foster a discussion about friendship, bullying, education, and the power of a positive self image. Quality discussions will help your child build his/her comprehension skills.

Here are a few questions to use when discussing this book.

1. What genre is this book, fantasy or realistic fiction?
2. Identify the the moral or lesson in this story.
3. How could Aria help other characters understand that they are special too?
4. How would you describe Aria's teacher?
5. Describe how Aria changed throughout the story.

WHAT DO YOU SEE WHEN YOU LOOK IN THE MIRROR?

"Some of life's greatest lessons show us that we've always had wings."

Katrina Denise

ABOUT THE AUTHOR

Katrina Denise is a mother, author, speaker and educator. As an educator and mom, she observed many children bypass books, because they could not relate or see themselves in the characters. After watching her four-year-old daughter select novels simply because the cover displayed an African American with natural hair like her own, she knew her passion for writing had turned into a need.

The Message in the Mirror is her first children's book, and aims to help young girls develop a greater sense of self, while realizing that beauty is more than skin deep.

CPSIA information can be obtained
at www.ICGtesting.com
Printed in the USA
LVOW06*1341081017
551658LV00017B/160/P